Published by Hachette Partworks Ltd
Based on the Mowgli Stories in *The Jungle Book* and
The Second Jungle Book by Rudyard Kipling.
ISBN: 978-1-906965-03-7
Date of Printing: November 2009
Printed in Singapore by Tien Wah Press

THE JUNGLE BOOK

Disney

H hachette

Deep in the Indian jungle, Bagheera the panther heard a strange sound. He discovered that it was a Man-cub! The baby boy was in a basket, which lay in a half-sunken boat on the river.

Bagheera felt sorry for the baby. He carefully carried the basket ashore.

"The Man-cub will never survive without a mother," Bagheera said to himself. Then he remembered that a wolf family lived nearby. Perhaps they would adopt the Man-cub.

Bagheera brought the basket to the wolves' den.

When the mother wolf and her cubs found the laughing baby, they smiled. Rama, the father wolf, was not so pleased at first. But soon he, too, was smiling at the Man-cub.

The wolves named the Man-cub "Mowgli."
For ten years, he lived happily in the jungle.
Mowgli learned many things from the
wolves: how to scratch himself, how to play
dead and how to run!

But one day, there was some terrible news in the jungle. Shere Khan the tiger had returned. The fearsome tiger hated all humans because a hunter had once shot at him. So Mowgli was in danger!

Late that night, the wolf pack gathered with

Bagheera on Council Rock. They decided that Mowgli must leave. Bagheera knew of a Man-village, where he could take Mowgli and where he would be safe.

But taking Mowgli to the Man-village would not
be easy.

"This is my home," protested Mowgli, as Bagheera
tried to pry him from a tree.

"I don't want to leave the jungle!"

Reluctantly, Mowgli began the journey to the Man-village with Bagheera.

Night began to fall. When they came to a big tree, Bagheera decided they would spend the night there. Bagheera gave the boy a lift up.

"Go to sleep," Bagheera told Mowgli, as they settled themselves on a branch.

But they were not alone. Kaa the
snake was hiding in the tree.
He thought Mowgli would make a
tasty treat!

Mowgli woke up and saw
Kaa. "Leave me alone," he said
to the snake.

"Do not be afraid,
Man-cub," said
Kaa. "Trussst me.
Go to sssleep."

Kaa stared at
Mowgli. Mowgli began to
feel dizzy. He was under Kaa's
spell. Kaa wrapped his long
tail around Mowgli.

Just then Bagheera woke up. He slapped Kaa
with his paw before the snake could hurt Mowgli.
Kaa fell to the ground with a THUD!

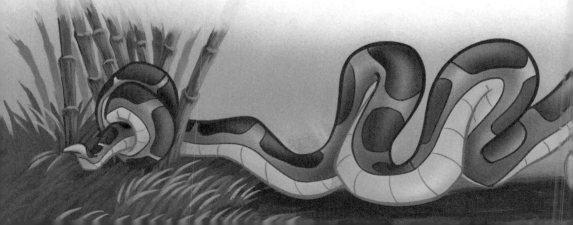

"You have made a ssserious missstake, Bagheera," said Kaa, as he slithered off.

Bagheera told Mowgli, "You see, the jungle is too dangerous for you. You belong in the Man-village. We will go there in the morning."

But Mowgli did not want to live in the
Man-village. So he left early the next morning.
"I can take care of myself!" said Mowgli to
Bagheera, as he walked away. "I don't need
anyone." But after a while, Mowgli felt lonely.

Then Mowgli heard
somebody singing.
It was Baloo – a big,
friendly bear.

"Well, hello there,
Little Britches," Baloo
said to Mowgli, with a
smile.

They quickly became
friends.

Baloo taught Mowgli how to dance like a bear...

... and growl like a bear...

… and even how to fight
like a bear!
   "I want to stay in the jungle
with you Baloo!" said Mowgli.

"I like being a bear," Mowgli told Baloo, as they floated down the river.

Neither of them noticed that several monkeys were watching them.

Before Baloo could stop them, the monkeys
grabbed Mowgli! They brought Mowgli to their
leader, King Louie.

"So you're the Man-cub," said King Louie.
"Crazy!"

"I'm not crazy. You are!" said Mowgli.

"Have some bananas," said King
Louie, shoving two into Mowgli's mouth.
King Louie struck a deal so Mowgli
could stay in the jungle. Then the
monkeys decided to celebrate.
Everybody started dancing.

Meanwhile, Baloo found the ancient ruins where the monkeys lived. In order to rescue Mowgli, Baloo disguised himself as a big monkey and danced right into the party.

Baloo's plan worked! While the monkeys sang and danced, he carried Mowgli out of the ruins.

"Thanks for rescuing me," said Mowgli. "I didn't want to be a monkey. I would rather be a bear, like you."

"But you are not a bear!" Baloo said sadly. "The jungle is too dangerous for you. You belong in the Man-village."

"You are just like Bagheera!"
shouted Mowgli. "I don't want to go to the
Man-village! I can take care of myself!"
So Mowgli ran away from Baloo, too.

Mowgli ran through the jungle.
Then he ran right into Shere Khan!
"Do you know who I am, Man-cub?"
asked Shere Khan.
"Yes. But I am not afraid of you,"
said Mowgli.

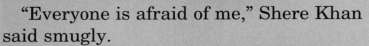

"Everyone is afraid of me," Shere Khan
said smugly.

"Well, you don't scare me," said Mowgli.

"Ah, you have spirit for one so small,"
said the tiger.

"You deserve a sporting chance.
I will close my eyes and count
to ten. It makes the chase more
interesting."

Shere Khan began to count.
But Mowgli didn't run away.
He wasn't about to be bullied by
the tiger.

This only angered Shere Khan. Just as he lunged for Mowgli, Baloo came to the rescue!

He grabbed
the tiger's tail
to try to save
the Man-cub.
Suddenly a bolt
of lightning
flashed in the
sky. The lightning
hit a nearby tree,
starting a fire.

Mowgli picked up a burning branch and tied it to
Shere Khan's tail.

There was only one thing Shere Khan feared:
FIRE!

He let out a roar and fled.

Bagheera and Baloo were so
happy to see that Mowgli was
not hurt!

"We're glad you're safe, Little Britches," said Baloo, when Mowgli ran up to the big bear and gave him a big hug.

Mowgli hugged Bagheera, too. He was happy to see his friends.

It was beginning to get dark, so they found a safe place to rest. Soon they were all fast asleep.

The following morning, the three friends walked to the river. Mowgli was explaining to Baloo and Bagheera how he could stay in the jungle – especially now that Shere Khan had gone away.

When they arrived at the river, they heard someone singing. They crept closer and saw a young girl fetching some water from the river.

"What's that?" asked Mowgli.

"Forget about those," said Baloo. "They're nothing but trouble."

Mowgli decided to take a closer look. The girl turned, smiled at Mowgli and dropped her jug of water.

"Hey, she did that on purpose!" Baloo said, from the bushes, as Bagheera nodded wisely.

Mowgli picked up the jug the young girl had dropped. He refilled it with water, waved goodbye to his friends and followed her into the Man-village.

"Mowgli will live in the Man-village from now on,"
said Bagheera, as they headed back into the jungle.
"We will miss him, but he is where he belongs."

"Yes," agreed Baloo, "but I still think he would
have made one swell bear!"